Presidential Popcorn:
The Spelling Beetle

Nadia Johnson

Presidential Popcorn: The Spelling Beetle
Copyright © 2020, Nadia Johnson

Illustrations: Mariah Green
Cover design: Mariah Green

ISBN: 978-1-952926-04-4

Printed in the United States of America

PeeWee Press, A Division of Manifold Grace
Publishing House, LLC
Southfield, Michigan 48033
www.manifoldgracepublishinghouse.com

Dedication

To my little brother and my older sister:
my inspiration and best friends.

Thank you for pushing me--literally pushing me--to
do my best. I couldn't have done this without you.

Table of Contents

Chapter  1: Trophies

Trophies. Big, sparkly trophies. When you wake up, what's the first thing you see? Your dresser? Your door? Your annoying little sibling in your face shouting, "It's time to wake up!" Well, when I wake up, the first thing I see is my sister's trophy case. It's literally overflowing with awards, certificates, and, of course, trophies. Anything from academic contests to fine arts competitions, from cook-offs to sports tournaments -- you name it, she's probably won it.

Now, when you go to brush your teeth, what is the next thing you see? Your sink? Your mirror? Your annoying little sibling, *again*, but this time they're shouting: "Why did you delete my *Karate Bob* recordings?" Actually, forget the last one. Only *my* annoying little sibling would shout that. Anyways, the first thing I see when I go to brush my teeth is my trophy case. And do you know what *my* trophy case is overflowing with?

NOTHING.

Well, that's not completely true. I do have some participation certificates stored up there. And I'm sure that a family of dust bunnies have burrowed on the bottom shelf. Oh, and how can I forget

Cardigan, my "Make-a-Moose"? He's my trophy case guardian and my huggable candy safe.

I always hide my gummy bears in his stuffing so George can't get to them. And yes, George is the "annoying little sibling" I was talking about. The point is, I was tired of looking at my empty trophy case. Seeing Cardigan sitting up there all alone just made me want to cry.

So, that's why I, Olivia Hudson, planned to make my trophy case so full that I would need another one. But, before I tell you how that all went down, why don't I introduce myself. As said before, my name is Olivia Marie Hudson: **Future President of the United States of America**--but you can call me Olive. If you're wondering how I, as a fourth grader, plan to raise money for my campaign, just know that I have a system.

Why don't we take an explanation break? Every month, my parents pick out a list of big words from the dictionary called "$5 Words." As an incentive to expand my vocabulary, my mom agreed to give me **up to $5** if I correctly use them every week. Those big words will come in handy when I'm writing my inaugural speech after I win the 2052 election. If you ever want to visit me, I live in the state of Virginia, the birthplace of most of the Presidents in American history; that includes George Washington, Thomas Jefferson, James Madison, James Monroe, William Henry Harrison, John Tyler, Zachary Taylor, Woodrow Wilson, and, one day, Olive Hudson.

I have two siblings: One older sister named Gabby, and one younger brother named George. That's right. I'm the middle child. If you would like to know more about your future president--like how her favorite food in the whole wide world is popcorn… specifically, lightly buttered with a sprinkle of salt and a hint of lime--why not just look at my "All-About-Me Poster"? I completed it just a few weeks ago and got an A+, not to brag.

All About Me Project!

Name: *Olivia Marie Hudson*

Age: *9 years old*

4ᵗʰ Grade

My Family:

Mom, Dad, Gabby, George, and Me

Birthday:

June 16

Hometown: Pearly Lane, Virginia

Favorite Food: POPCORN!!!

Favorite Movie: Chronicles of Cabbage

Dream Job: Being the President of the U.S.A

Now, back to my story. Where was I? Oh, I remember. *This* is how it all went down...

It was a sunny Saturday morning, and I was peacefully sleeping in. However, I immediately woke up when my little puppy Pow-Wow jumped right on my tummy. Before I realized what was going on, he began covering my face with doggie licks. "Well, good morning to you too," I said as I lifted Pow-Wow off me and pushed him to the floor. He started barking happily as he did his "*Time for breakfast!*" dance. Then, the sweet smell of cinnamon filled the room.

"Mmmmm. Gabby must have made her famous cinnamon waffles for breakfast," I said as I walked over to my calendar and crossed off that day. There were only a few more days until our class Spelling Bee! I slipped on my "presidential" eagle slippers along with my fuzzy pink robe and picked up Pow-Wow. I held him in my arms as I walked down the hallway. But as soon as we hit the stairs, he jumped out of my arms and hopped like a leapfrog all the way down. I laughed as I saw my "speedy pup" zoom past me.

"Mornin' Sis," I yawned as I entered the kitchen.

"Good morning, Olive. I made waffles!" Gabby smiled as she flipped one on a plate. When I went to sit down, I was surprised to see George looking in the mirror to make sure he looked okay. He was wearing his khakis and a nice blue polo shirt to go with them. Did I mention his hair was already combed?

"Hey, George. Why are you wearing your church clothes?"

Completely ignoring my question, he came over to me and asked, "Can you help me buckle my belt?"

"Olive, come and get these waffles before they get cold!" Gabby snapped.

"Okay I'll be right there -- wait a second." I looked at the counter and saw a *nutmeg* jar instead of a *cinnamon* jar. I gasped. "Gabby! Did you make these waffles with nutmeg instead of cinnamon?"

"Um, yes," Gabby answered.

I gasped, *again*. "How could you?!"

"Whatever, Olive. We ran out of cinnamon and nutmeg was the substitute. Plus, they taste the same."

I gasped *a third time.*

"Will you stop that?" Gabby yelled.

"I'm sorry. I just prefer *cinnamon waffles* to be made with *cinnamon.* And if you don't know,

cinnamon and nutmeg definitely do not taste the same. I'm practically a connoisseur when it comes to high quality breakfast food," I said as I sipped my orange juice. *Connoisseur* is one of my "$5 Words" and it basically means someone who knows a lot about something or has good taste.

"Fine! If you don't want my waffles, then eat cereal!" Gabby shouted.

"Then I guess I will!". I reached for the top of the fridge where all of the cereal was and grabbed the box of *Fruitie Cubes.* I poured myself a bowl and gasped *a fourth time.*

"Olive!" yelled Gabby.

"Okay, I promise that was my last one. But look!". Hysterically, I pointed to the cereal.

"What seems to be the problem now?" Gabby asked, clearly annoyed.

"Can't you see? These are *Fruitie* "spheres" not *Fruitie Cubes!*" I exclaimed. George and Gabby looked at each other and then rolled their eyes at the same time.

"Well, Drama Queen—I mean Drama *President,* here are your options for breakfast:
A. stop complaining and eat my waffles or
B. settle for a cup of Pow-Wow's puppy
   chow."

"Yuck! Stinky mutt pellets for breakfast? I am not *that* desperate," I said as I shoved a spoon of

Fruitie "spheres" -- not cubes -- in my mouth.

"Really? Because your breath smells like you ate two servings of Pow-Wow's stinky mutt pellets." George snickered.

"Ha, ha. Very funny George. You just wait until I move into the White House. I will make sure that there's not a single pinch of nutmeg in my waffles. I will make sure that every single *Fruitie Cube* is a cube and not a sphere or any other geometrical shape. Give me liberty or give me--"

"A break! Now eat your cereal," Gabby interrupted. Pow-Wow did his "Amen, Sister" bark.

"Well, I'm off," George said as he walked toward the door. His blue polo shirt was covered with milk stains and waffle crumbs; his face was smudged with sticky syrup, and his belt was yet unbuckled.

"And where do you think you're going?" I asked.

"Before mom left to go to the store, she said that I could go to Rigley's house after breakfast."

"GASP!" I shouted. George and Gabby both glared at me. "What? You said not to gasp any more. But you never said I couldn't say, 'Gasp!' Anyway, you let mom go to the store and you didn't ask her to bring back cinnamon? How could you? Gabby, I thought we were sisters!" I exclaimed as I splashed my spoon in my milk.

"George, why are you going to Rigley's? Is that why you're all … well, somewhat dressed up?" Gabby said while handing him a napkin. She gave him the, "*Wipe your mouth*" look.

"She has this super cool club going on and she let *me* be the president… *Olive!*"

I immediately spat the milk and cereal out of my mouth. "You? The President? Look, buddy, I don't mean to crush your dreams, but I'm the future—"

"Not the President of the U.S.A! The President of Rigley's club! It's called Bean's Bugs Beyond, or the *Triple B Club* for short," he explained.

Let's take another explanation break. Rigley Bean is our across-the-street neighbor, one of George's best friends, and a second-grade businesswoman. She's always trying to start a new business and find ways to fill up her piggy bank. Her dad used to run a bug extermination business called, "*Bean's Bugs Be Gone,*" and for some reason she decided to open a club called, "*Bean's Bugs Beyond.*" All I knew was that it most likely had something to do with the giant bug field in her backyard.

"The Triple B Club? You know, I'm going to open a club too. It's going to be called "The W.W.C. Club": Waffles with Cinnamon Club. Everyone except for *Gabby* is welcome to join."

Gabby gave me a grim look. "Just let it go."

"No, Gabby. People like Elsa from *Frozen* 'let things go.' But people like me, Olive Hudson, enjoy eating CINNAMON waffles!!!" Then, Pow-Wow did his, "*Preach it!*"bark.

"Speaking of clubs, Rigley wants you to be the vice president of it. Pretty cool, right?" George piped up.

"More like 'pretty cool' wrong! First of all, I am not going to be the vice president of a *bug* club. Second of all, I don't care what club it is. I am not going to be a *vice* president. It's 'President' and nothing but 'The President'. Sorry," I said as I ate my last bite of *Fruitie Cubes* -- I mean *spheres*. Just know that when I get the money, I'm suing the company. What?!! First, they mess up the shape and then they make the cereal without the artificial food coloring that turns your milk purple! Okay, I didn't make such a big deal about that before because honestly, that's kind of gross. But I expect *everything* that's advertised on the box!

"Oh, come on Olive! Please? We get to do all sorts of fun things. We get to read comic books, drink *Whiz-Bang* crème sodas, and go into the legendary bug field and see some pretty cool bugs. You even get a free trophy!"

"Trophy? A trophy?! Did you just say--"

"Trophy? Yes, I did. So, if you become the vice president of the Triple B Club, then you get a big, sparkly trophy." *Olive Hudson: Vice President of the Triple B Club.* Had a nice ring to it, key word: *had.* Never let your little brother draw you into something through a trophy. No matter how big, or sparkly.

"I don't know George. It's going to take a lot of thought. Hey, Gabby? Do you have a trophy for being a vice president?"

"No, but--"

"Then it's decided. I'm in. And after I win this trophy, I'll fill up my whole trophy case. It will be so full that I'll need another one. Cardigan, dust bunnies, prepare for more—"

"You done, yet? 'Cause as President, I got places to go," George said while looking at his watch.

"Sorry. Got caught up in the moment. But you know that Rule #29 does say, '*Success is the best!"* You're probably wondering why I said, "Rule #29." Well, when I was in second grade, my Aunt Joanna gave me the official copy of *110 Rules of Becoming the President.* And I've been using it ever since.

Quickly rushing up the stairs, I started going over some speeches that I could say. For example, going over the issue of not being able to wash powder puff paint out of your favorite pair of jeans. Or not being able to clean dog poop off your shoe with hand sanitizer. Or why hand sanitizer only kills 99.9% of germs instead of 110%.

Anyway, I was upstairs zipping up my presidential, I mean *vice* presidential red dress when I heard George scream, "Let's go, Olive! This President is not going to stay good looking for ever!" Rolling my eyes, I headed back downstairs.

But before I could make it to the kitchen, Pow-Wow came like a super-sonic peanut and tripped me. I fell and bumped into the table which caused syrup covered NUTMEG waffles to spill all over me. "Pow-Wow! Now I look like George!" I shouted while syrup dripped from my hair.

"That's *President* George to you," George corrected as he began to walk out of the house. Even though I was sticky with syrup, I began to make my way toward the door. Then Pow-Wow blocked it so that I couldn't leave until I promised that he could go with me.

"Sorry, boy, but we both know that you'll just eat up all the bugs and then fertilize the comic books. I could sneak you home some crème soda to drink. I heard that every dog that drinks crème soda can fly. Of course, we never see them because they fly up, up, up and then turn into fireworks. And I did not name you Pow-Wow because I wanted you to explode. So, it's probably best if you stay here." Gabby shook her head in confusion, but Pow-Wow jumped on me and gave me an *"Alright"* lick.

Out the door, covered with breakfast, I was going to inspire many bug loving children: every girl's dream -- other than becoming the President, of course.

Chapter  2: Triple B Club

We finally made it to Rigley's house and surprisingly, there was a giant line waiting outside.

"I have to tie my shoe. You can head in and I'll meet you there," George said, while stooping to tie his glow-in-the-dark *Teenage Mutant Ninja Turtle* gym shoes. I walked in front of the line, but I was suddenly stopped by the grim sight of my sworn enemy.

How 'bout another explanation break? You might be wondering why I have a sworn enemy. Well, it all started back in kindergarten when **someone** stole my design for my popsicle stick sculpture, took all the credit for it, and won the classroom art show. Plus, she got a stuffed panda AND IT WAS THE LAST STUFFED PANDA IN THE CLASSROOM PRIZE BOX! That panda was rightfully mine. I had a name for it and everything. *Moo-moo.* That was my name for it. *Moo-moo the Panda.* Now, I know what you're thinking. "Moo-moo" sounds more like a name for a stuffed cow. Well, I was really attached to naming animals after the sounds they made, and I wasn't sure if pandas made any noise. So, after singing "Old McDonald had a Farm" at circle time, I assumed that if the cow goes "moo", the panda goes "moo" too. It was going to be me and Moo-moo the panda against the world. But that's another story for another time.

"*Emily*?!" I exclaimed.

"*Olive*?!" she replied, but with a sneering look.

"*Emily*? Wait, I already said that."

"What are you doing here?"

"No, what are *you* doing here, at Rigley's *Bug* Club?" I asked, extremely confused.

"Well, you may not know, but Rigley let me be the manager."

"But this is still a *Bug Club:* A club which girls like *you* do not tolerate!" I said while leaning toward her. She was sitting at a table covered with posters that said, "*Triple B Club Registration: $1 and 6 Tic-Tacs per person (Entrance Fee).*" Every letter was in black marker and looked like whoever wrote it was in a rush. It was also covered with sloppy sketches of bugs. Obviously, the artist behind the poster was either a first grader or someone who was not very fastidious. That means that they did not pay attention to detail. The writing wasn't neat, and the bugs looked more like blobs than bugs. *Fastidious* is another one of my "$5 Words," by the way.

"Rigley said that she would give me $2 every twenty minutes I managed her club." Then, she pulled out her bedazzled hot pink clipboard and pointed to the paper clipped to it. "You see, *Olive*," Emily said to me as if I was a baby. "If I were to work for a whole hour, I would receive $6. Now, the only way I would get $6 is because twenty minutes goes in one hour three times meaning--"

"I know how to do math, *Emily!*" I snapped. She flipped over her clipboard and showed me all of her work.

"Sorry, but it's hard not to show and explain your work when you've won the *Math Olympics* three years in a row," she said while rubbing the paper in my face. Whenever Emily has the chance to brag about herself, she always takes it. I snatched the paper out of her hand and forcefully placed it on the table.

"Well, it was not so nice catching up with you, *Emily*, but I have a club to lead," I said while walking past the table, but I was stopped by Emily's evil clipboard.

"Hold your horses! If you can't read, this poster says '*Entrance Fee*' not '*Entrance: FREE!*'" she said as she slammed her clipboard on the table.

"Entrance fee?"

"Yes, *entrance fee*. And there's no cutsies, so... back of the line!"

"Excuse me! You may not know, but I'm the *Vice President*. That's right! I'm practically in charge of this joint!" I said proudly.

"No, *I'm* in charge. And I'm sure the *actual* vice president would not use syrup as hair gel," Emily said as she pointed to the hard flakes of syrup stuck to my ponytails.

"The point is, *Emily*, I shouldn't have to pay."

"Welllllll" Emily started as she flipped through the papers clipped to her clipboard. "Your name's not on the list, meaning you have to pay like everyone else! It's not personal, it's business. Now stop being annoying and get to the BACK OF THE LINE!!!"

"Wait. What list?" I asked. Then, Emily ripped a paper from her clipboard.

"*This* list! The V.I.B list! And you're not on it!"

"That's probably because I'm on the *V.I.P* list."

"No, *V.I.B* is *V.I.P*, but the 'B' stands for 'Buggie' instead of 'Person.' 'The Very Important *Buggie* List.' Everyone on it comes in for free. YOU ARE NOT ON IT!!!" she shouted.

"Why not? I'm the **vice president!**" I shouted back. The people in line behind me became restless in their waiting. I plopped myself on the ground. "Until justice is served, I shall take part in a nonviolent protest. I'm not moving until my voice is heard".

"We've already heard enough! Listen, Olive. I'm not going to get paid for arguing with you. You can either pay up or go away! I suggest you choose option #2," Emily replied. Meanwhile, George in his finally tied *Teenage Mutant Ninja Turtle* gym shoes walked right pass me into the club. I quickly jumped up and grabbed the clipboard from Emily's hand.

"Hey! George isn't on the list! How come he doesn't have to pay?" I asked, upset.

"He's the President. He automatically gets in for free," she explained.

"But I'm the *vice* president!" I whined, stomping around like a preschooler having a tantrum.

"Yes, you're the *vice* president. Which means you're not the president. But if you want to be on a list so badly, there's room on the V.A.B list: 'The

Very Annoying Buggie' list. And look! You're the first one on there and you only have to pay half the price," Emily smirked while holding her hand out. I rolled my eyes and fished in my pockets for something equivalent to $1 and 6 *Tic-tacs.*

Now that I think about it, charging only $1 and 6 *Tic-tacs* was not wise on Rigley's part if she was planning on paying Emily $2 for every twenty minutes she managed her club. Not to mention, she still had to replace the money spent on all the crème sodas and comic books if she was expecting a handsome profit. And since Emily spends most of her time lowering people's self-esteem with her unnecessary fashion criticism and insults in general, paying her to be the club's manager was more of a liability than an asset. In the world of business, a *liability* is something that puts you at a disadvantage while an *asset* is something that puts you at an advantage. Those aren't my "$5 Words". I just read about them in one of my dad's business books.

All I was able to find in my pockets was a few sticky pennies and a half-eaten bag of *Cheddar Bunckins.* However, Emily was willing to let me in...*finally.*

"Oh, and don't forget to hang up that stack of

posters before your big speech!" she called out behind me.

"Speech? But when do I get my--" But before I could finish, I bumped into Rigley who was wearing a pink skirt, a purple shirt with a heart on it, and a headband with colorful ribbons hanging from it to hold up her afro of brown curls.

"Oh hey, Olive! Didn't see ya there. I didn't know you wanted to join my club," she said smiling.

"Oh, I didn't *want* to join. But I agreed to be your Vice President - if, and only if, I receive a big, sparkly trophy," I said, still wondering why I hadn't received it yet.

"Yes! I almost forgot. But what's the rush? We have a lot planned for opening day and it all starts off with your speech. Here, put this on," Rigley said as she handed me a fluffy gray fake beard.

"You want me to wear that? No way!"

"Oh please?! Since you're giving a speech, this beard will make you look wiser."

"I'll make the speech, but I won't wear the beard," I said, folding my arms.

"That's too bad. I just finished polishing your trophy. But if you still don't want to wear the beard..." Rigley persuaded as she waved the beard like a flag. At first, I thought about how ridiculous

I would look. But then, I began picturing how happy my poor, lonely Make-A-Moose, Cardigan, would look once I brought home a big, sparkly trophy to fill up some of the emptiness of my very empty trophy case. I wouldn't be doing it for myself, I would be doing it for Cardigan and the dust bunnies who still haven't paid rent for burrowing in my trophy case. Long story.

I selflessly snatched the beard out of Rigley's hand and said, "Okay, fine."

"Good. Now, you're up in five minutes. Don't be late!" Rigley then did her little "*cute clementine*" smile and frolicked away. I still can't believe a second grader was able to run her own club. I begrudgingly put on the scratchy, old beard as Rigley invited both me and George onto her porch-stage.

"Girls and gentle-boys, welcome to my official Triple B Club! But before I go on, I would like to invite Vice President Olive to the stand." The audience was completely silent, but that only made it easier to hear the crickets applauding for me. Even with a bear of a beard on my face, I still walked confidently.

"My dear children, we, right now, are the generation of the present. But soon, we will be the generation of the future: The future of cleanliness and organization. So why is it that our hand sanitizer bottles say that they kill only 99.9% of germs? That 0.1% is the reason America sees trouble. But I say, let's be the generation that adds back 0.1% to everything that will make America great again. Amen, my brothers and sisters. Amen."

At first, everyone just sat there and remained silent. Suddenly, they began to roar with laughter. I never thought the topic of hand sanitizer was so comical. They were all probably too young to understand the gravitas of the issue. *Gravitas* is another $5 Word and basically means serious-ness. Rigley then ran on stage, letting the audience know that the bug field was officially open.

"Wow! They love you," she whispered to me as we watched the members of the club roll on the ground busting their guts with giggles.

"I'm surprised with their response. I didn't even have to pull out my rehearsed joke!' I said happily.

"I knew the beard would help! I'm so glad Emily convinced me to have you wear it."

That's where I pulled the plug. She can put me on the *V.A.B list* all she wanted to, but there is no way I was going to let her get away with humiliating me in front of an entire club, especially when I'm the vice president of it.

"Hold up. You're saying that if it weren't for Emily and her big mouth, I wouldn't have had to wear this thing? Well, forget her! She may have won this time, but I still look amazing in this beard.

In fact, I think I'm going to wear it every time I make a speech from now on," I said as I began to braid my new *speech beard.* "Actually, this thing is pretty hot and itchy. And everyone knows that the best speeches are presented by people who are comfortable." But as I tried to pull off the beard, I realized it was stuck to my face. I pulled, and tugged, and felt as if I was trying to rip off my skin.

"Um Rigley, this thing won't come off," I said trying to forcefully remove it from my face.

"Oh, that's because I put super glue on it," Rigley said, as if that wasn't a BIG DEAL.

"YOU DID WHAT?!!!" I exclaimed. Everyone looked toward me and began to laugh even more.

"Well, Emily suggested that I put glue on it so that it looks more realistic. People don't trust phonies, you know." At that point, I was burning with anger, which probably wasn't good because I'm pretty sure the beard was flammable.

"Rigley, as *vice president,* let me give you some advice: STOP LISTENING TO EMILY!!!" I shouted.

"I can't! She's the manager!"

"*Manager, Smanager!* Her favorite color is pink, so how about you give her a pink slip!" If you don't know, you give someone a pink slip if you are going to fire them. I was confident that the whole subdivision had been watching me. I stomped off the stage and headed toward the exit.

"Nice beard, *Olive.* Surprisingly, a girl like you can really pull the look off. Or I guess you can't pull it off since I heard it's stuck to your face," Emily snickered. I would've come back with a sick comeback, but I was too upset that I sacrificed chilling at home all day for all of that foolishness. "I was just wondering what you were bringing for special show and tell this week," she called after me. I paused.

"Special show and tell?" I whispered to myself.

"It's this coming Friday. You know, along with the Spelling Bee. I've been practicing for a whole month, which probably wasn't necessary since I won the Spelling Bee last year without even taking one look at the list." I rolled my eyes. Again, whenever the *"Queen of Boasting"* gets a chance to present herself, she takes it. "I'm going to be bringing my authentic orange karat tiara. And by karat, I mean the diamond, not the vegetable. My aunt is the Duchess of Winnipeg Meadow and gave me her tiara for my birthday. I'm sure that I'll have the BEST special show and tell ever to be seen," Emily said cheerfully as she hugged her clipboard.

"That's what you think. But I have an even more

amazing show and tell than that. In fact, the President thinks so himself," I said, trying to sound confident even though it was obvious I was lying.

"Really? Then what is it?"

"You'll just have to wait and see. Hence the name *show* and tell."

"Olive, come quick! I have something I need to show you. *Vice President and President's eyes only!*" Rigley shouted from the bug field.

"Oh, did you hear that, Emily? *Vice President's eyes only!* Not the snobby, overpaid manager's eyes. My eyes," I chanted while I attempted to *Moonwalk.* I tripped, but that didn't dim my confidence. There was just one problem: I needed to find a special show and tell that was 1,000 times better than Emily's, plus approved by the President all by Friday. But what's more awesome than a tiara that's worth a zillion dollars? I ran over to The Bug Field with George and that's where I found the answer.

"Behold!" Rigley exclaimed. "The catch of the day!" She slowly unscrewed the peanut butter jar near her foot. "This is Peanut Butter." But what was inside was not normal peanut butter. Instead, it was a furry, creepy-looking, orange and black Goliath tarantula looking me dead in the eyes.

"Um, I think this spider ate all of your peanut butter!" I whisper-screamed as fear crept down my spine. Even George looked a little freaked out.

"No, *Peanut Butter* is his name. That's because I caught him in this peanut butter jar," Rigley said as she let the tarantula crawl out of the jar and onto her hand. "He's a 'best friend spider' meaning he's both an amazing companion and a personal bodyguard that bites your enemies."

"Enemies? I wonder if Emily is allergic to spider bites," I thought as the spider continued to catch my interest. But then again, if that was the same spider that gave *Spider Man* powers, then Emily would be able to shoot webs at my face and swing around school. No way was I going to give her that opportunity. But if the spider bit me...

Duh-nuh-nuh-nah!

It's your friendly future president

Spider-Olive!

But then again, if I were that type of superhero, I would probably not be able to control my powers and end up crashing into a wall, or get tangled in my own webs, or accidentally shoot them in my mouth. Yuck! Personally, if I was like *Spider Man*, I would swing on string cheese instead of spider webs.

"Now, as Vice President and President I'm giving you guys the responsibility to look after the new club mascot for a whole week."

"Cool!" George and I exclaimed with excitement. Though he lived in an actual peanut butter jar, that tarantula was the answer to having the best special show and tell ever. And since it was the best show and tell ever, I just knew I was going to get a trophy. Not only that, since George was the president of the Triple B Club and agreed that the tarantula was super awesome, then I could truthfully say, "*The president himself approved of my show and tell.*" And I think you and I can agree that a tarantula that bites your enemies is 110% waaaaaay better than a tiara, by far.

"That was the answer to having the best special show and tell, EVER."

Chapter  3: Pterodactyl with a Capital "T"

Friday had finally come and I knew that this was the day I would receive another trophy by winning the class Spelling Bee. What's even more exciting is that I was able to get the beard off of my face! I zipped up my presidential red dress, grabbed Peanut Butter's jar, and ran down the stairs. George and I were taking care of the tarantula in shifts. I knew it was George's turn, but I needed to present Peanut Butter for special show and tell. So, as I walked to the kitchen, I was careful not to show the jar to him. I also hid the tarantula from Gabby since she can't stand spiders, or basically anything with eight legs. That even includes an octopus.

I looked at the spelling list one last time and set Peanut Butter's jar down on the table. "With efficiency, Olive! The bus is going to come soon, so fill up on breakfast," Mom said while grabbing George's lunch out of the fridge. The word *efficient* means to get the job done without wasting time.

35

You guessed it. That's another one of my "$5 Words."

I grabbed a bagel and the jar of actual peanut butter out of the cupboard. I love peanut butter bagels and why not enjoy one before my big victory? As you can see, doing that was not the wisest thing to do since the jar of actual peanut butter from the cupboard and the jar with Peanut Butter, the tarantula, inside looked the same!

George, being his helpful self, put the peanut butter jar away for me. There was just one problem: It was the wrong jar. That's when he realized I was trying to sneak out the spider during his shift. "Hey! It's my turn to watch Peanut Butter!" he shouted, still placing the wrong jar in the cupboard.

"I know, but I need him for special show and--" Just then, the school bus came.

"MOM!!!" George shouted. I quickly placed the *actual* peanut butter jar into my backpack, shoved my bagel in my mouth and ran outside, with my list of words in hand.

"Love ya!" I muffled, since my mouth was still full of bagel. I looked over my words on the bus ride, just so I wouldn't forget anything. "Let's see. *4th Grade: Easy, 4th Grade: Average.* Aha! *4th Grade:*

Difficult. Pepperoni: P-E-P-P-E-R-O-N-I. Alright! I've got this Spelling Bee in the bag! And by bag, I mean lunch bag," I said since I had packed myself a slice of pepperoni pizza for lunch.

"Next word," I said while flipping through the pages in the packet. "*Humility*." Right when I read that out loud, I remembered I had just learned about that word in church on Sunday. The lesson was all about how God wants us to put others first and to not glorify ourselves.

"Humility? Why, I'm so humble I should receive an award for my humility," I thought to myself. "*Then* I would really have more trophies than Gabby!"

I would have checked on my special show and tell—not knowing that it was actually sitting in my cupboard—but I didn't want to draw a lot of attention. So, I just sat back and enjoyed the ride.

At school, everyone entered the room with butterflies in their stomach since our class Spelling Bee was only moments away. No one really paid attention during Math since we were all focused on spelling words in our heads. Then, *it was time.* We all jumped to the front of the classroom in a single file line. Mrs. Sippi, the world's coolest fourth grade teacher, had us go through a *Practice Bee* before we began. Nobody got out, which made me a little nervous. I was standing first in line since it was probably best for the winner of the Spelling Bee to spell the first word.

"I can do this. I. Can. Do. This," I said to myself, confidently.

"Olive, your word is... *'Pterodactyl.'*"

"Pterodactyl?! What kind of *4th Grade: Easy* word is that? I remember going over words like *'temperature'* and *'terrible,'* but not *'pterodactyl!'* I thought to myself, breathing heavily. "No! I can do this! I. Can. Do. This. When in doubt, just sound it out," I told myself. I remember George used to have a whole book on exotic dinosaurs like the pterodactyl. I probably should have paid more attention to the spelling.

"*Pterodactyl,*" I repeated slowly. *When in doubt, just sound it out.* "T-A-R-A-D-A-C-T-I-L. *Pterodactyl!*" I was confident that I spelled it right, until I saw all of my classmates faces. They looked as though I spelled the word "*milk*" wrong.

"Sorry, but that's incorrect," replied Mrs. Sippi.

"What?!" I exclaimed.

"*Pterodactyl* is spelled P-T-E-R-O-D-A-C-T-Y-L. Lucas, your turn."

"Incorrect?!!! But Pterodactyl doesn't start with a P! It has a 'tuh' sound!" I cried.

"Olive, please sit down," Mrs. Sippi said sternly, so I knew she was serious. "But it's not fair," I whimpered as I returned to my seat. However, it wasn't over yet. There was still special show and tell to get through and I *would* find a way to get back into the Spelling Bee. Emily may have won that time—and the time before—but I still had a better special show and tell than her...or so I thought.

After the nerve-racking anticipation of the Spelling Bee, we all gathered in a circle to present our show and tells. Emily ended up coming in first place in the Spelling Bee; Henry, one of my best friends, got in second; and Reggie, my other sworn enemy who was also part of the popsicle stick sculpture scandal back in kindergarten, got in third. But I was in first place for sounding things out!

Starr, another one of my best friends, presented her show and tell first. She brought her new monster truck skateboard which was decorated with purple flames. Then Emily went with her karat tiara, which surprisingly interested the majority of the class. I asked Mrs. Sippi if I could go last since I wanted to be the grand finale.

"Ladies and Gentlemen. In this jar I hold Virginia's finest spider. This tarantula is both a companion and a personal bodyguard. Some may say that it's related to the spider that gave *Spider Man* powers." That got everyone's attention.

"Did you just say tarantula?" Emily asked with disgust.

"Olive that does sound pretty awesome, but I said no pets allowed," Mrs. Sippi replied.

"But *Peanut Butter* isn't a pet. He's a *best friend spider*," I replied back as I began to unscrew the top. "Here he is!" I said as I showed the class the open jar.

"Um, Olive? I think your spider turned into actual peanut butter," Emily snickered. Then the whole class started to laugh.

"What do you mean?" I asked as I looked inside of the jar. It only took me a few seconds to realize that I grabbed the wrong jar!

"Well, that was a very… um… interesting show and tell--" Mrs. Sippi started.

"No! My special show and tell wasn't supposed to be a nutty bread spread! I really did have a tarantula! My brother must've accidentally put his jar in my cupboard!" I tried to explain. But that didn't quiet the laughter.

Everyone settled down once Mrs. Sippi got up and said, "Alright. Put your show and tells in your backpacks and pull out your Social Studies books, please." So far, that day was one of the worst days ever. However, it wasn't going to stop me from finding a way back into the Spelling Bee. After Mrs. Sippi dismissed for lunch, I stayed back a little longer to have a chit-chat.

"Oh Mrs. Sippi! I got something for ya!" I said as I walked toward her desk. She was wearing her alphabet earrings, you know, for the *Spelling* Bee. She also looked as though she was just about to enjoy the colorful fruit salad, topped with a puffy layer of whipped cream, on her desk.

"What's up?" she asked as she jabbed her fork into a juicy pineapple chunk.

"Well, I was wondering, since *pterodactyl* was such a 'fast pitch' and advanced word, if you could, maybe, let me back into the Spelling Bee?". I waited for my answer. You'd think the world's coolest fourth grade teacher would say "yes," but she didn't. "I had a feeling you'd say no," I said as I reached for the paper in my pocket. "So, if you let me back into the Spelling Bee, I'll give you this free coupon." I handed Mrs. Sippi the paper and she began to laugh.

"*Give Olive no homework for a whole week,*" she read aloud. "How exactly is that supposed to benefit me?"

"Because, then you'll have one less person to grade for a whole week! And in your free time, you can use this," I said as I fished for the other piece of paper in my pocket. Once I found it, I handed it to Mrs. Sippi. "*Mother-Daughter Spa and Frozen Yogurt Day. Enjoy 2 free Snazzleberry Twists after 50% off mani-pedis.*" Well, this surely sounds nice, but I don't have a daughter. Four sons, but no daughters."

"I would happily be your substitute daughter for

the day! Just get me back in the Spelling Bee and I'm all for it!" I said, hoping *that* would change her mind.

"Sorry, Olive. I would love to have you as a substitute daughter but--"

"I feel ya. My sister thinks that you can substitute nutmeg for cinnamon," I said as I grimaced at the past event. "My brother has a whole book on dinosaurs. All of them have names that are less hectic to spell than *pterodactyl.*"

"Sorry, Olive, but rules are rules. Once you're out, you're out," she said, popping a blueberry into her mouth.

"Well, how about a trip to Paris? You can see the Eifel Tower and everything! Just slip me back in the Spelling Bee and--"

"Wait. Paris? Paris, France?"

"Paris, France? Of course not! I was talking about *Paris, Idaho.* My Grandma Judith lives down there and her neighbor is a potato farmer." Mrs. Sippi looked disappointed.

"But you said that I could see the Eifel Tower," she said while scooping the rest of her salad into a plastic bowl.

"*Eifel?* Well, I meant *awful,* as in the *'Awful Towers'* of hay and manure."

"Sorry, Olive. But hey, there's always next year. Now get to lunch before you get hungry. Strawberry for the road?" she asked, handing me a whipped cream covered strawberry.

"No thanks. Me not winning the Spelling Bee made me lose my appetite," I said sadly as I walked out of the classroom with my lunch box.

Surprisingly, I was the only one with a lunch box since everyone in the school ordered mushroom soup for lunch. Everyone, *except* for me. It's not that I forgot, or just don't like mushroom soup. It was the new lunch lady that was the problem.

You see, every third Friday of the month, our former lunch lady Mrs. Jones always made her famous mushroom soup. But a few weeks ago, she retired, and we got a new lunch lady: Mrs. Joans.

Her last name is spelled J-O-A-N-S instead of J-O-N-E-S like the last name of our former lunch lady. That Friday was the third Friday of the month Mrs. J-O-A-N-S made mushroom soup, and I wasn't ready to try it. Only Mrs. J-O-N-E-S makes good mushroom soup, at least in my opinion. But it seemed to everyone else that the new Mrs. Joans' soup tasted just as wonderful.

"You know you forgot to order," Jazzy, my last best friend, said. She, Henry, Starr and I were all sitting at a table together. I was the only one without mushroom soup. I sniffed the air and was shocked that such a savory aroma was coming from their bowls. *Aroma* is another "$5 Word" and is used to describe something that has a wonderful scent. Even though the soup smelled delicious, I was loyal to Mrs. J-O-N-E-S and didn't regret bringing my lunch from home.

Completely ignoring Jazzy's comment, I interjected, "PTERODACTYL?! Ooh! When I become President, I'm going to erase every word that uses unnecessary silent letters from the American Spelling Bee! And now I know why it's called the 'Spelling Bee'. Because you can easily get *stung* by ridiculous words! You know what doesn't sting? *Butterflies.* Everyone knows that butterflies are way better than bees. I would much rather be in the Spelling *Butterfly* or even the Spelling *Beetle.* B-E-E-T-L-E. See! I can spell the word *beetle* because *beetle* is a 'fourth grade: easy' word, unlike PTERODACTYL!" I ranted.

"Did she let you back in?" Starr asked, slurping her soup.

"Did the king of England accept the colonists' last peace effort through the Olive Branch Petition in 1775 right before the Revolutionary War?" I asked, annoyed.

"Um... no?"

"NO! He did not. And no, Mrs. Sippi did not let me back into the Spelling Bee and I'm fresh out of ideas. Ooh! I've got it! Henry, you've been in the

Spelling Bee every year. How about you let me take your place in second and--"

"No way! I've come in second to Emily almost every year and I plan to beat her in the Grade Bee this Monday! If I don't win, my dad is gonna make me go to the zoo with my cousins. And I can't stand the zoo. I especially detest the penguin exhibit," Henry said while shuddering.

Last explanation break. Everyone has something that makes them feel a little uncomfortable. For some, it's speaking in front of people. That, of course, does not include me. For others, it's the dark. But for Henry Chu, it's penguins. It's not because they smell like fish or look like they wear tuxedos. It all started in second grade on our field trip to the zoo. Our class got the opportunity to meet Poppy, "the tap-dancing penguin". Before we headed over to the penguin exhibit, Henry and the rest of the people in my travel group grabbed lunch from one of the restaurants on the zoo's campus. I had a double-decker-lasagna-burger with a side of cheese fries, while Henry decided not to be adventurous and eat boring fish sticks. Since he wasn't able to finish in time, he decided to take them "to-go" by carrying them in his pocket. That was a big mistake. It wasn't long after we entered the exhibit that Poppy, along with the other penguins, began to chase him all around and peck at his pockets to try and eat his fish sticks. The signs specifically said not to bring any food into the exhibit, but Henry unfortunately learned that the hard way. On the bus ride back to the school, people sang, *"Henry Chu got attacked at the zoo by a bunch of penguins and cried, 'Boo-Hoo!'"*. As Henry's best friend, I was the only one who did not join into the teasing ... no matter how hilarious the event was.

"Sorry, Olive. I have to win. Think of the penguins!" he cried.

"Well, aren't you a pterodactyl!" I snapped as I grabbed my lunch box and walked away.

Chapter ⭐ 4: 1st Place "Sounder Outer"

The teasing about my special show and tell seemed interminable. I don't mean to be annoying with my "$5 Words", but as said before, I'm saving up for my campaign come the 2052 election. Anyways, you can use the word *interminable* to describe something that goes on and on without end. Unfortunately, Mom soon found out about the "switch- a-roo" and made George and I return the tarantula to Rigley. But before we could, Peanut Butter escaped!

That's right. First, Gabby found him in the cabinet not too long after George and I left for school. I imagined Gabby accidentally eating him on her toast, thinking he was *actual* peanut butter. Thankfully, she told me that he got away. George and I looked all throughout the weekend for Peanut Butter, but we couldn't find him anywhere. I wonder if he's been going on little adventures around the house. Maybe he's living in a shoe under George's bed. Maybe he's fallen in love with

51

another tarantula named Jelly. Peanut Butter and Jelly. Isn't that cute? Rigley didn't think so when I explained everything to her. Can you believe she impeached me from my position as Vice President and banned me from the club for losing the club mascot, even though it wasn't entirely my fault? I mean, forgive and forget people!

Anyway, it seemed all hope was lost for the Spelling Bee until Monday, the day of the Grade Bee, came. I walked into the classroom and was surprised to see that no one was there. So, as a mature fourth grader, I sat my stuff down and quietly took my seat. Then, Mrs. Sippi entered the room.

"Good morning, Mrs. Sippi. Where is everybody?" I asked as she walked to her desk.

"I'm just as lost as you are. A lot of students seem to be missing from the other classes too. The traffic wasn't bad when I left out." Suddenly, the email alarm on her computer went off like an ear shattering siren. Almost sixteen emails had come to her in nearly ten seconds. "Oh, my goodness!"

"What is it?" I asked as I walked over to the desk.

"This is astonishing! It looks like a lot of people are absent since they're still recovering from the symptoms of the stomach flu. They must have caught a bug over the weekend or something."

"Stomach flu? How did everyone get the stomach flu?" I asked. Then, it hit me. *The mushroom soup!* I knew there was something fishy about it! Like I said, only Mrs. J-O-N-E-S' mushroom soup is good, and it seems that my opinion was proven fact.

"But what about the Grade Spelling Bee?"

"Well, most of Mrs. Thompson's fourth graders are here, but I think we'll have to cancel it today."
"Cancel it? Don't do that! With Emily and everyone else gone, I, by default, am in first place for the Spelling Bee! Yes!" I shouted as I danced around the classroom. "I'm in first 'cause I ate pizza, but I'm still in first!" I sang happily. "Do I get a trophy? Or a certificate?" Mrs. Sippi grabbed a certificate and wrote my name on it.

"Because of the stomach flu, by default, Olivia Hudson will take Emily Watson's place in first," she said while handing me the certificate.

The Grade Bee did end up being rescheduled, but we got to do a Practice Bee and the winner actually got a trophy. Learning from my past experience, I decided to go last.

"Olive, your word is '*Tyrannosaurus*'".

Tyrannosaurus? As in TYRANNOSSAURUS REX?!! Again, with the dinosaurs?!! When I become President, I am going to erase every dinosaur name or word that has something to do with the Jurassic time period from the American Spelling Bee. Of course, I DID NOT spell that correctly, meaning I DID NOT win the trophy and I LOST the Spelling Bee -- AGAIN!

At that point, I felt like crying. I had finally gotten another chance and I blew it! I didn't mean to be a sore loser, but it's kind of hard not to be one when your sister's good at EVERYTHING! Well, everything except for telling the difference between cinnamon and nutmeg.

"All I wanted was one trophy. Just one!" I said to myself.

"All I wanted was to prove to the whole world that I was just as amazing as Gabby. Maybe even a little *more* amazing. If I just had more trophies than her, everyone would cheer for me instead of *'Little Miss Perfect'.* Is that too much to ask?!"

The rest of the day was pretty boring. I had to join Mrs. Thompson's fourth grade class because

Mrs. Sippi had a doctor's appointment. The bus ride home was even more miserable since everybody wouldn't stop singing *"Diddey Money"*. That's a song by this pop artist named *Purple Fang,* who can't sing, but makes bank off of making world's craziest songs. I bet she has many trophies, even though her voice sounds like a dying camel!

> *"Diddey Money one more time*
> *Don't want your pennies or your dimes*
> *I stole your heart and you broke mine*
> *Oooh, my Diddey Moh—Nay!!!"*

They sang over and over again. I was ready to take off my sock and shove it into their mouths to stop all of the racket. Luckily, we pulled in front of my house just in time.

"Guess who got an A on her science test?" Gabby said happily as I walked through the door.

"Let me guess. YOU? Well, that's no surprise," I snapped as I ran up the stairs.

"What's the matter with you?" she asked, and I replied by slamming my bedroom door.

"No slamming doors!" Dad shouted from his room. I pretended not to hear him and flopped on my bed. I looked up at my trophy case, then at Gabby's. I snatched the Spelling Bee certificate from my backpack and placed it right next to Cardigan. Then, I ran downstairs to do my homework.

An hour later, I was on the couch studying for my history test when Gabby shouted, "Olive, come quick!"

"I'm trying to bury my failure neck-deep in cookie dough ice cream, if you don't mind!" I shouted back. Dad let me have a scoop after dinner.

"But George is messing with Cardigan! And eating all the gummy bears!" Hearing this, I set my ice cream bowl on the table and ran upstairs.

"I'm coming to save you, my moose!" I shouted as I burst into my room. When I got inside, I was shocked at the sight of my trophy case. "Okay, either I ate too much ice cream, or Gabby switched trophy cases with me because all of those golden beauties weren't there before!" I said, as I gazed upon my now full trophy case.

"Surprise!!!" George and Gabby sang as they jumped from behind my closet door. Pow-Wow was doing his "*Surprise!*" bark along with them. "These are all yours," Gabby smiled. I could tell that they were all *her* awards, but they were covered with sticky notes with writing on them.

"Well, read them!" George said while handing me a trophy.

"*Best Big and Little Sister Award?*" I read as George handed me another one. "*Future President' Award, 'Ambassador of Speeches'*

Award, 'The Like- A- Boss' Award, 'The Food Critic' Award," I read on and couldn't help but smile. "Guys, this is awesome!" I said while hugging them.

"That's not all," Gabby said while grabbing another trophy from the closet. "Rigley told me that you forgot your trophy at her club, you know, before you got impeached for losing her tarantula. I felt like it needed some adjustments." I read the sticky note on it.

"Olivia Hudson: 1ˢᵗ Place Winner of the Spelling Bee. But I didn't win the Spelling Bee."

"Oh, I can fix that." Gabby grabbed a marker and wrote *T-L-E* at the end of the *Bee* in *Spelling Bee.*

"Spelling *Beetle?* What's that?"

"It's a new spelling contest and you won first place for spelling words by sounding them out. I present to you the *'When in Doubt, Just Sound It Out' Award,"* Gabby announced while applauding.

"Gabby, why would you do this?"

"Well, I figured that *my* trophy case was getting a little full. Plus, one of the coolest people on Earth deserves more than a participation award."

That's when the word *humility* came to mind. Even though I had learned about it at church, I had totally forgotten the true meaning of such an important word. I was so busy comparing myself to my sister and trying to prove I was the best that

I forgot what truly mattered.

Going through life trying to glorify yourself will leave you as empty as my trophy case was before Gabby filled it. But living to please our Creator is way better than any award or medal a person could give you.

"Since Cardigan can't fit in your trophy case now, ya think we can maybe…" George leaned close to me.

"Go ahead." And we all enjoyed the root beer, lime, cherry, and bubble gum flavored gummy bears inside.

The End!

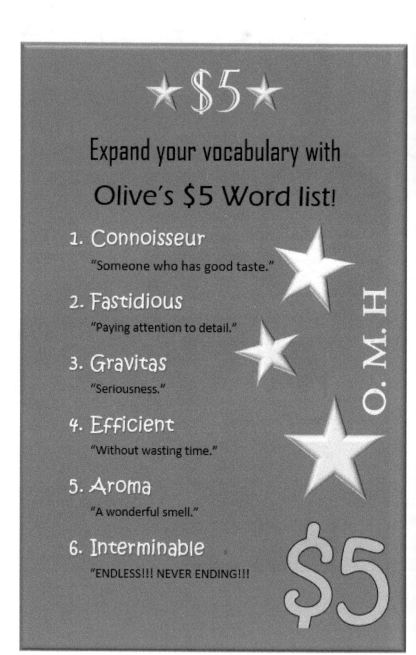

Meet the Author:

Nadia Johnson

Nadia Johnson is a 15-year-old author and composer from Belleville, Michigan. She has been writing songs and stories since the age of five. As the middle child, Nadia loves to spend time with her older sister and younger brother, along with expressing herself through the fine arts. Nadia dreams to perform and write musicals for Broadway and does not let her age stop her from pursuing the plans God has for her.

You can contact her via:
nadia.johnson@novamediapublishing.com

Meet the Illustrator:

Mariah Green

Mariah Green is a 16-year-old illustrator born in Detroit, Michigan. She began drawing at the age of 3 and went on illustrating books ever since. She has won many awards for her outstanding work.

You can contact her via:

ramiyahcreative@gmail.com

Acknowledgments

First, I would like to thank my Lord and Savior Jesus Christ for providing me with this opportunity to be a light unto others.

Next, I would like to thank my family, especially my parents, for supporting me in my endeavors and for encouraging me to follow the plans God has for me.

I would also like to thank Mariah Green, my friend and illustrator, for bringing my vision to life.

Lastly, I would like to thank Ms. Cheryl Andrade. Not only has she encouraged me not to wait to pursue my talents, but she has also been a great help in many of my other projects.

CPSIA information can be obtained
at www.ICGtesting.com
Printed in the USA
BVHW050138210721
612416BV00002B/491